Not Again, Annie!

Not Again, Annie!

Tony and Jan Payne

Illustrated by Rosie Reeve

Dolphin Paperbacks

First published in Great Britain in 2004
as a Dolphin Paperback
by Orion Children's Books
a division of the Orion Publishing Group Ltd
Orion House
5 Upper St Martin's Lane
London WC2H 9EA

A catalogue record for this book is
available from the British Library

Printed in Great Britain by
Clays Ltd, St Ives plc

ISBN   1 84255 158 2

www.orionbooks.co.uk

This is especially for Emma and
her Donkey of the Month, Chokky

T&J P

contents

Granny, Grumbler and a Great Day Out.

Gran's always saying that she doesn't get out enough, but last week I saw her in the garden, digging potatoes and building a garage, so she's not indoors *all* the time. She's just always complaining.

I thought she deserved a treat anyway.

Gran looks up at the sky every time she pegs out washing, so I know she's really interested in planes. I thought I'd take her to the air show at our local airfield. Of course, Gran would have to pay to get us in, but it was my thoughtful idea. I asked old Mr

Kravitz who lives next door to Gran if he'd like to come as well, so she'd have someone her own age to sit down with. Old people sit down a *lot*.

"You is very good girl!" said Mr Kravitz. He was really pleased by my kindness. "I was flying plane in Second World Wars. I have not even been to airport since fifty years."

Mr Kravitz speaks funny English.

"How are we going to get to this airfield?" Gran asked me. "Can Bizzy Lizzy take us?"

Bizzy Lizzy is my mum. Her name is Elizabeth really, and she's always busy. Actually, she's always busy somewhere else.

"I think she's in India," I said. "She

won't be back until tonight. And Dad can't drive. We could go on bikes," I suggested doubtfully.

"What, with my legs?" Gran asked. "Not likely! We can go on Grumbler. Grumbler can take Mr Kravitz as well."

"Oh no, Gran!" I said. "Please, not Grumbler . . . Double please . . . Anything but *Grumbler*."

Hundreds of years ago, Granny was given a motorbike for a wedding present. He's big and stinks and really loud. (It's definitely a 'him', by the way.) He goes *brackkkk* when you start him up and then he roars and grumbles, so Gran calls him 'Grumbler'. You can't hear yourself shout over the noise. He's covered in oil and gets red hot, like you're sitting on a chip pan. Grumbler's really scary. He's sort of *fun* too.

But Gran's driving isn't.

"Don't be such a wuss," she said. "Grumbler's out in the garden. Help me get the manure out of the sidecar." Grumbler has a funny little Wendy house thing on one side called a sidecar and it's just big enough to sit in. Gran has painted flames all over it to make it look cool. It rattles a lot and bits fall off and I always have to go in it, because I'm not allowed on the motorbike itself.

Gran went in to change and came out

looking really *grannish* – I mean, as only Gran can. She doesn't wear a granny-dress or granny-specs or granny-jewellery like ordinary grandmothers. This was *my* gran, and she was wearing a leather coat with a belt and a leather helmet with earflaps and goggles.

★

It took *forever*, but we finally got to the airfield (inside a huge cloud of smoke). When we could see again, the airshow looked a complete load of nothing. Most of the planes were in a field not doing anything; they were just *parked*. Some of them had *two* sets of wings, like they were from *ages* ago, and they were painted in really, really, dull colours – greeny brown and browny brown, all splodged on anyhow. We'd come to see *real* planes – Harrier jump jets and Airbuses, Stealth Bombers and Concorde, stuff like that. What we actually got was garbage out of the skip and old planes looking as if they could do with a good wash!

One or two planes were up in the sky, but the drivers were rubbish too. They couldn't even fly in straight lines and some were having a hard time keeping the planes the right way up. One of the drivers had totally lost it, going over backwards in circles with his engine on fire, blowing out red and blue smoke from the back. Then old Mr Kravitz

saw a big brown plane with fans on its wings.

"Look!" he cried. "Look . . . is *Dakota*. That is plane I flew in war! I, Flight-Lieutenant Jerzy Kravitz, First Class. Six flying medals – one for swimming. Four lengths! Must go see." He went up the steps and disappeared inside.

There was a man standing in front of the Dakota plane. He asked Gran if she wanted to go up as well and she told him all about her arthritis and I got bored and started counting railings. Then he asked me if I was having a good time and I told him what I thought of the planes and their drivers.

"If I was that bad at driving planes," I said, "I wouldn't be flying in front of all these people. I'd go someplace where there wasn't anyone who could see me . . . and *practise*!"

The man laughed and said I should talk to his drivers because they needed someone like me to put them straight.

Another man came up then and said, "Who's your friend?" Meaning me, I suppose. The first man said, "This is . . ." and stopped, so I told him Annie Fidgen and he said, "This is Miss Annie Fidgen and I'm putting her in charge of all you pilots. She thinks you need more practice."

Well, that was amazing! Perhaps the air show wasn't such a flop after all. Anyway, they seemed very happy about it, laughing and everything, and one said, "Let's go and get something to eat."

As they walked away, the second man turned round and called out, "As you're in charge now, you'd better get someone else to fly the Dakota. I just quit. Why don't you ask the old man sitting in my seat if he wants the job?" And they both laughed again.

Gran had wandered off, but I found her under the plane, poking tyres and things and muttering and I heard the word 'thirsty'.

"I'm going to look in the driver's room," I told her.

"Don't be long," she said. "It's nearly Happy Hour. Drinks are half price in Happy Hour."

I climbed up the plane's steps and went inside. There were two seats in the front and *two* steering wheels, with the tops broken off, and a big window to look out of.

Mr Kravitz was in the nearest seat. He had a huge grin on his face, even *before* I told him he could fly the plane if he wanted.

"This country wonderful," he said. "I never think to fly again. Did man really say I could fly plane? You will have to help me, Annie. Is long time."

"Oh yes," I said. "I'll help you."

Mr Kravitz was so happy! He couldn't stop touching the knobs and things and turning little dials above his head. Luckily there was a book of instructions on the dashboard, but I had to read it out to Mr Kravitz because he can't read English. There were lots of drawings with arrows on them and some really long words that we haven't done at school yet, so I didn't bother with them. There were still plenty of small words I knew. He nodded as I read the instructions and pressed some buttons and the engines went putt putt and then started with a roar like Grumbler.

While Mr Kravitz was looking at the pictures some more, I went to find Granny in

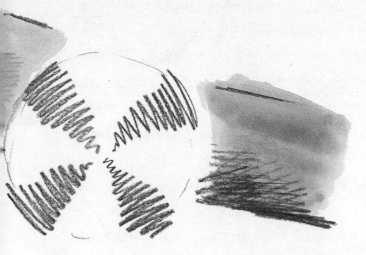

the beer tent. I had to drag her out and *push* her up the aeroplane steps, still clutching her glass. She dropped into the other driver's seat like a sack of cement, but she didn't spill anything. I strapped her in and told her Mr Kravitz had been given the driver's job.

Then we took off.

We flew just above Hertford Road. I wanted to see if Jessica Jolly was in her garden, but the plane's bonnet was in the way.

Then Mr Kravitz got his boot caught in the pedals or something and we flew sort of sideways for a bit and I could look down, because we were going round in circles on edge. I flew over Jessica Jolly's house *four times* but didn't see her. Then Mr Kravitz got cramp and when he freed his boot, had to bang his foot on the floor, "To get blood going again."

When we were flying in a straight line again, Gran said she needed the toilet and went to look for one. She was gone such a long time, I was worried she'd locked herself in, so I went to look for her.

I had a surprise when I got next door. The plane was full of people! They were all on one side of the plane – due to us flying sideways probably. If I'd known we had passengers, I'd have put the seat belt sign on. If there was one.

Everyone was looking at Granny with their mouths open. She was standing in the middle of the seats, giving the safety demonstration. You have to do that in planes with passengers.

But Granny can't see that well and she was saying, "The emergency exit doors are *here* and *here*." She pointed to the sides, except she was pointing to the toilet and a grey metal locker and then she blew a whistle and pulled a cord and the life jacket round her neck blew up and she fell over.

One woman said, "We only came inside the plane to clean it!"

I managed to pull the blown-up lifejacket off Gran's head. It squeaked a lot and she was yelling, "Stop that! My ears are coming off!" And when we finally wrestled our way up off the floor, she had a really red face and her hair was sticking straight up like a scary wig!

I hauled Granny back into the driver's room again and she calmed her hair while Mr Kravitz looked for somewhere to land. We saw an airfield. Gran said it must be Southend.

We landed brilliantly! It was probably the most exciting landing the passengers had ever had. We hit the ground and bounced right up again, over a house and a lorry and then another plane, and bounced some more and then we stopped. OK, we were on the grass, but it was near the runway – just a short walk, really.

I thought old Mr Kravitz was amazing, going straight into bouncing and leap-frogging planes on his first practising day when he hadn't even been *in* a plane for fifty years. The passengers couldn't wait to get off and when they did, they started hugging each other and laughing and crying and kissing the ground and other weird stuff. One man yelled

out that they were going to stay there for ever. All of them were. They didn't want ever to come back.

They must have really *loved* Southend.

It might have been because there was a show on. Lots of red-and-white striped cars and trucks came screeching to a halt beside the plane, going ner-ner, ner-ner, and flashing blue and red and yellow lights like real emergency cars. It was great fun. Really

colourful. People were dressed up like fire-
fighters and police and stuff and straight away
they started chatting to the passengers.
Everyone was looking at us and pointing, and
we smiled and waved. I'd have liked to have
gone out to join the fun, but we couldn't stay.

"We'd better take the plane back to the
man," I said. "He'll be wondering where
we've got to."

Mr Kravitz drove back on to the concrete
bit of the runway. The cars and fire engines
drove along beside us and they were honking
and beeping and there were more behind us,
flashing lights. What a send-off! Southend
probably doesn't get many visitors.

When we got back to our airfield, it was nearly dark and almost everyone had gone home. Mr Kravitz didn't do any more leap-frogging, but he showed us how he could fly right through the beer tent and up again without touching the ground.

"Would have fly better with glasses on," he said, when we finally got down on the ground. "Next time will bring glasses."

On the way back to the car park, we passed a man closing up his ice-cream stall. He told us that a plane had been stolen. There'd been a big hoo-har and the police had only just left, he said!

Well, that might have been a *bit* exciting, but not as exciting as our day out, I bet.

When Grumbler finally dropped me off at home, I thought I'd probably get a telling off.

It was way past my bedtime.

My Granny is from Outer Space

I got into trouble at school this week.

We had a lesson called 'Creative Writing'. Miss Felton said to write a story. It could be about anything we liked, as long as it was *creative*.

 I wrote a story about a boy called Simon, who had a film showing up his nose. All his friends would come to his house

and look up his nose to watch the film and Simon was really fed up because it was one of his favourites and he was the only one who couldn't see it, not even with a mirror.

Well, I thought that was really creative, whatever Miss Felton said. She read it and said to do it *again* and asked why I couldn't write something nice, like other children, about pet rabbits and stuff. So I wrote about my gerbil, Beckham, who had this film showing up his nose. Miss Felton sent me out of the class.

When I was allowed in again, Miss Misery said I couldn't go on the school outing to the TV studio, which was in two days' time. I wasn't really worried. I can always get my own way with teachers. I just act like somebody good and *nice* for a while — because teachers like good, nice little girls, like *Sophie Rednap,* who is pretty and wears frilly dresses. Mum says I can be pretty when I want to be, but I never do. She says I frown all the time and it puts people off, but Sophie Rednap smiles *all the time.* It's not natural.

Dad says my smile is on upside down, that's all.

Anyway, next day I wore my pinkest, frilliest, horriblest dress and shoes with flowers on. I said, "Yes, Miss Felton, thank you, Miss Felton." I smiled all day and I worried in case the smile stuck and I couldn't NOT smile ever again. Still, I was pretty and nice, even though I didn't feel like it, and Miss Felton said I could go to the TV studio after all, just as I knew she would.

A studio is where they make TV programmes like Blue Peter and stuff. Watching Blue Peter is like going to school when you don't have to, except the grown-ups are not teachers, they're real people, and they show you how to make finger puppets from rubber gloves and train your dog not to do its business in people's front gardens. I was hoping the rock band Live Ants With Dead Heads would be there. They're all girls and their singing is pathetic, but they set fire to their instruments and smash them up on stage, so it's really good. Beckham likes them too, actually. He gets really excited when they are on.

The studio is right in the middle of town and our mums were supposed to take us. *My* mum wasn't around, as usual. She was in America, begging for old buses she could take to Africa – else she would have taken me, I know. Gran had to take me on Grumbler.

The TV studio was big and boring, but most of the front was one enormous window and even from outside you could see

that TV lady with the teeth. You know, the one who tells you the weather. She was pointing at a big map and there were other people around with headphones on, taking no notice.

A lady in a pullover came to the entrance and took us upstairs to a room with only chairs inside. She said that Julia Prescott, the lady who does the evening news on TV, wanted to see us. Julia Prescott is famous, Miss Felton told us, and she was quite nice, but I don't know any news and I didn't know her. She told us we would be watching the making of an episode of *My Family's from Outer Space*.

I've seen it on TV. It's stupid. It's all about some children who find out they're not from Wimbledon, like they thought, but came with their

mother
from
another
planet. I don't actually
believe someone's mother
from another planet can look so
much like Kylie Minogue.

I wasn't really listening to Julia
Prescott; I was looking out of the big
window. You could see for miles over
the rooftops but, looking down, there
was just a big empty car park. Well, empty
except for Gran and her motorbike.

They were going round in circles, really
fast. You couldn't hear anything through the
thick glass and you could hardly see
Grumbler at all because of all the smoke he
was chucking out. I don't know how Granny
was steering, standing on the saddle like that.
She gets so bored when she's waiting around
for me.

"And this is the control room," said the
pullover lady, as I marched in behind the
others. I didn't know what was happening

because my brain hadn't been paying
attention. I was thinking about Gran having
fun when I wasn't.

In this room the floor sloped up to the back
and at the top was a big desk with knobs on.
Through a window at the front, but still
indoors, you could see a whole house and
garden. It was lit up with bright lights, but it
looked as if the walls and the roof had blown
off, because you could see everything inside.
Kylie-Minogue–Mum was doing acting in

one of the rooms and you could hear what she was saying, even though the window was in the way.

It was *sort of* interesting, watching a TV show being made, but it was so *ordinary*. It was supposed to be about aliens, but it was more like *EastEnders*, and it was hard to understand what was going on. Kylie-Minogue-Mum wasn't talking to anyone, but spoke to thin air as if somebody stood in front of her. "Oh, Juno …" she wailed, "I've almost forgotten what it's like to eat real food. When was the last time we ate Swamp Spiders and … and …"

"Jollup Grubs!" a man with headphones on reminded her.

"When was the last time we ate Swamp Spiders and Jollup Grubs? I hate it here, Juno. When can we go back to Xaarg? … Really, Jerry, do we have to say this rubbish?"

After a pause, the headphones man turned and looked up at our window. "It's not working, is it?" he said.

"No!" I called out, and then clamped my

hand over my mouth, because I suddenly thought he probably wasn't talking to me, but to the man at the desk with the knobs. The man didn't mind though. He smiled at me (Miss Felton didn't!) leaned forward and spoke into a microphone.

"You're right, Jerry, it doesn't work. The script is weak and the stunt man playing Juno, the alien monster, still hasn't turned up."

A lady with a clipboard said, "I think he has, Mark. I've just seen him. He's already in a leather monster costume, doing wheelies in the car park. He's good! I didn't know you could do wheelies with a *sidecar*."

"Well, get him up here then. And make it quick!"

What a laugh! They thought Gran was a stunt man. And while we waited for the lady to go and get her, Mark was muttering to himself about 'the script needing something *different'*. He looked at us and said, "Got any ideas?"

The other kids just shrugged, but I put my hand up. Miss Felton tried to stop me, but I pretended not to see her and told the man how he could make his story more different.

He looked really surprised and then he smiled. "That's brilliant! A gerbil, eh? Brilliant! And a film showing up its nose? Great! Any idea where we can get a gerbil at short notice?"

"Yes," I said and I took Beckham out of my pocket.

But just then the doors to the studio opened and the clipboard lady came in with Gran, who was still wearing her leather coat and her flying helmet with the flaps over her ears. She really looked like something from another planet, but she must have been roasting!

"Get someone from Make-up," Jerry said. "The body is all right but it needs a better head. Bring the green monster head with the dripping slime. This one's too red and it looks a bit like a woman."

I could see Gran was getting really crabby and just as she was about to give Jerry an earful, he put his arm round her shoulders and said, "I hear you came on an old motorbike. That's brilliant! This is what I want you to do. You are a hideous monster from the same planet as Mrs Suet," he told her, pointing to Kylie Minogue. "And a friend of hers. You've been searching for her through space and now you've found her ... I want you to burst through the garden wall on your motorbike, trash the garden doing stunts like you were doing in the car park, then jump off the bike, run along the top of the wall, climb the drainpipe, crash through the lounge window and hurl yourself on top of Mrs Suet ..."

Gran looked at the spiky wall she was
supposed to run along and the drainpipe she
was to climb, and the lounge window she was
to crash through. "Right-oh," she said.

The people from Make-up put a knobbly
green rubber mask with pop-out eyes over
Gran's head and perched the leather helmet
on top. What a riot!

Granny really got into the part and I could
see she was enjoying herself, especially when
she smashed through the greenhouse. She was

riding Grumbler with one hand on the handlebars, one foot on the seat, and the other arm and leg waving in the air. She also knocked over some cameras and drove through the kitchen, but nobody minded. They said it was 'Brilliant!'

Then it was my turn, being the gerbil trainer. But, actually, Beckham was no good at acting. He skulked in the corner with his bottom pointing at the camera, and when I saw the finished programme later, on TV, they'd used a cow instead, probably because

cows like looking into
cameras and they've
got bigger nose
holes to look up.

The TV people gave
me two free tickets to see
Live Ants With Dead Heads,
who are doing a gig in the studio next week.
They'll probably seem a bit tame now after
Granny, but I'm looking forward to going.

And even though he doesn't *deserve* to go
with me, and is in disgrace ... so is Beckham.

Donkey of the Month

I'm rich! This is how I did it.

It was my birthday and Dad said I must have a party because that's what little girls have, even when they don't want one. Dad thinks he has to make up for Mum always being away. Dad's all right really ... but he's embarrassing sometimes. (Normally you don't notice him much, but sometimes he goes a bit crazy.) Last year he made me invite six or seven friends to our house, even though he knows I don't *like* my friends, and he thought it was a really funny idea to stand on the table and drop spoonfuls of jelly on our plates from a long way up. Then he did his magic tricks

and then I had to open my presents in front of everyone.

OK, I got *some* cool presents, but I got rubbish presents too, and Jessica Jolly was secretly laughing at me. I know she was.

Gran had made her present for me, as usual. A dog kennel I think it was, but I wasn't sure because it had windows with little curtains and pictures on the wall and anyway, we don't have a dog. Still, it was better than getting something

she'd *knitted*, because although Gran can *start* knitting, she can't stop, so she knits until the wool runs out. Sometimes clothes end up fitting me and sometimes they fit elephants.

Mum's parcel came from South America – Bolivia, actually – and in it was a thick, hairy, blanket thing, but stiff and spiky like a door mat, with a big hole in the middle to put your head through. There was a hat of the same stuff, but with a bobble on top and earflaps. How would you like to wear clothes like that in front of people?

This year I told Dad I'd
quite like not to have a party
... Well, actually, I said, "If
you make me have a party,
I'll hold my breath until I
go blue and die and
you'll be sorry." I
hadn't tried that since
I was five, but it still works.

So I didn't have a party.

I had a *donkey*.

Our house lives in a place called Enfield,
which is on the outside of London. London is
really all joined-up houses without any grass
and trees, but it ends at Enfield and then there
are fields and stuff. There is a donkey
sanctuary there. This is where donkeys go
when they are fed up. For my birthday, Dad
adopted one for me. I was really pleased.

"Where are we going to put it?" I asked.

"You won't actually keep the donkey here,
Annie," Dad said. "The people who run the
sanctuary look after her for you, but you can go
and see her any time and the donkey will send

you a birthday card."

Well that didn't sound like much. "What's the point of having a donkey if you can't make loads of money giving rides to people?"

"That's not the point, Annie. It's to help sad old donkeys who have no one else to love them. Your donkey doesn't even have a name, because no one loved her enough to give her one."

Yeah, well . . . all right then . . .

I went to see Gran, just in case *she'd* got me something I'd like, but it was only a scarf. A *giraffe* would have tripped up over it, it was so long. She was in the kitchen. Her hands were bright red right up to her shoulders from making this year's elderberry wine, and her mouth was bright red from drinking last year's.

"Had to make room in the bottles," she said.

She'd been busy in the garden too. It used to be just dirt, but it was all grass now. She'd used those little bits of field you can buy to put on the ground like carpet tiles – turves, they're called, and they make a lawn in five minutes. We went outside to look.

"It gives me somewhere to sit out, and I can keep an eye on Mr Kravitz," Gran said. "He's not very well at the moment. He's got the flu."

Mr Kravitz came out of his house to say happy birthday, but then he started making weird noises into a hanky. "Is not problematic," he said.

Problematic. That was a new word – I liked it. I waved and ran home. I didn't want to catch his germs.

Next day Dad took me to see the donkey. We went on the bus. The sanctuary was a nice place. It smelled of donkey-doos, but that wasn't problematic. There were lots of donkeys. *My* donkey didn't do much, just stood there looking droopy with her head down. I gave her three Polo mints and an apple that the lady in charge gave me to give her. Then we went home.

After a few days, I started wondering if my donkey was all right. She was a *bit* nice – she didn't want to sit on my lap or anything, like some animals – plus I worried she was standing out in the rain, getting a chill. I got Dad to take me again and this time I took my own treats. She was really pleased to see me, although she pretended she wasn't and looked at my shoes all the time. But when I gave her some Polo mints and asked if she liked them, she nodded her head, so she's clever for a donkey. She brays, which is a really funny noise,

just like old Mr
Kravitz made
when he
had flu in
his hanky at
Gran's, and she

looks a lot like him too, so I started calling her
Mr Kravitz.

I went every day. I went in a taxi, because
Dad didn't want me going on the bus on my
own. Soon everyone at the
sanctuary was calling her Mr
Kravitz too. She's
got lots of
personality
once you get to
know her, even if
only her ears move and
nothing else.

One day, there was a
notice that said GOOD
HOMES WANTED FOR
DONKEYS. I went to the
lady in charge, Mrs

Smiley, and told her I had a good home for one. "That's excellent, Annie," she said. "Are you sure your parents have enough space for a donkey?"

How much space could one small donkey need?

"It's not problematic," I told her. "My gran has and it's all new grass."

"Well, we'll just check with Gran, shall

we?" said Mrs Smiley. "We must get a grown-up's permission. Do you have her number?"

We went to her office and she rang Gran. "Mrs Weatherburn?" she asked (that's my gran's name. It's not Fidgen like mine), "I have little Annie in my office. I'm ringing to find out if you have enough room on your grass for Mr Kravitz . . . You have? Good . . . I have to check, you understand . . . That's excellent . . . New grass, too! That's just what Annie said . . .

"Well now, Mrs Weatherburn, I'm not sure  a drop of elderberry wine *would* 'buck him up', as you put it. A few oats, perhaps . . . Yes *oats* – half a bucket every morning ... By the way, Mrs Weatherburn, Mr Kravitz is a lady."

I couldn't hear what Gran was saying until then, but I heard her now. *"HE'S WHAT?"* she exploded.

I got Mr Alexander – Lizzie from school's dad – to pick up the donkey in his van. OK, it was an ice-cream van and it was a bit difficult. We couldn't turn off the loud-speaker jingles, so every time we stopped, people came up to buy ice-creams. Then they'd see the donkey's head sticking out and shriek and spook poor Mr Kravitz. But we finally got her to Gran's in one piece.

Gran seemed surprised to see the donkey, but she got a free tub of Super-Whippy ice-cream and a chocolate flake, so she didn't mind, I don't

think. She had trouble with the name though.

"Mr Kravitz, come out of there!" I heard
her yell. "Mr Kravitz! LEAVE MY HEDGE
ALONE!" And she ran down the path,
waving a broom.

Old Mr Kravitz – the *real* Mr Kravitz – was
stooping down behind the fence and he shot up
looking really guilty. "I not touch hedge! I not

near hedge. I planting chrysanthemums in pot."

"Not you, Mr Kravitz, *this* Mr Kravitz."

"Oh. The horse is Mr Kravitz too? Is amazing coincidence!"

After a few days it got a bit problematic. He got fed up rushing out of the house every time Granny yelled at the donkey and so closed all his windows so he couldn't hear her.

I put up a notice in the front garden:

DONKEY SANCTUARY.
Unhappy Donkeys Cared For Here.
A. FIDGEN, PROPRIETOR.

I copied it from a sign I'd seen at the sanctuary. I thought people would bring all their old fed-up donkeys to be looked after, but I don't think there can be many in Enfield. I didn't get any. I did get four hedgehogs though. People put money in a box I left outside Gran's door as well. After two weeks I had one hundred and forty-seven pounds and a peanut.

But that wasn't how I got rich.

Gran complained that she couldn't sit out on the lawn any more, because the donkey had eaten it. I asked her to order some hay instead. I didn't mean for her to get a whole haystack! And when it was piled up in the garden, Mr Kravitz just stood with her head in it. She didn't move for eight days.

Other things were problematic too. A few days ago I had to scrub out the ice-cream van because Mr Alexander kept slipping on something nasty. The neighbours complained about the smell.

Then I had a visit from Mrs Smiley while I was at Gran's.

"Just thought I'd drop by to see how Mr Kravitz is doing," she said. "Where's the field? Is it nearby?"

"Mr Kravitz is in the back garden and she has her own haystack to eat and she's got room to turn around and everything, but she doesn't want to."

"Dear me!" said Mrs Smiley and she swept

down the passage and out through the back door. "I thought your grandmother had a *field*?"

Mr Kravitz was still standing with her head in the haystack, so you couldn't even see her ears move. Mrs Smiley smiled though, and said, "Well, I can see you've taken good care of her, she's put on weight since I last saw her. She's really made a mess of the garden, though. I think we'd better have her back, don't you think?"

"I suppose . . ." I said.

When Mrs Smiley collected the donkey, I gave her the hay as well. For nothing. I didn't charge her anything. I just gave it to her.

I had a card later, "Dear Friend, I thought you'd like to know that Mr Kravitz has been made 'Donkey of the Month'. There was a little rosette stuck to it and it was signed by Mrs Smiley.

When I showed it to old Mr Kravitz next door, he thought it was for him and he's taken it away and put it on his mantelpiece. He's tickled pink. He thinks he's Donkey of the Month.

I was quite sad when the donkey went away, but when she'd gone, I wrote another notice and put it outside, over the old one:

HEDGEHOG SANCTUARY.
Unhappy Hedgehogs Cared For Here.
A. FIDGEN, PROPRIETOR.

Well . . . I still had hedgehogs to look after, didn't I?

People brought more hedgehogs (and more money) to Gran's,

 and I had to get a bigger money box to put on the step.

But that wasn't how I got rich.

I'd put up a new sign:

**DONKEY POO.
£1 A BAG**

That is how I got rich!

Snot Soup.

It was a week before our school's Open Day.

Open Day is really atrocious because *parents* come and we have to show them what we've done in class. We have to point out which are our paintings on the wall and show our books and answer stupid questions. We run egg-and-spoon races and three-legged races and there are races for mums. Except my mum was in China, telling off their government for the way they look after chickens or something like that. Anyway, she couldn't come this year.

And there's the competition. Everyone hates it. Four teams fighting for a rubbish prize. Like a *book*.

"Pay attention, class!" said Miss Felton. "This year's competition for Open Day will be 'Foods of the World!' Then she looked around, all excited, like she expected we should be interested.

Who cares about food? I don't. Food is put on a plate in front of me and I eat it, even if I don't want to. Sometimes my dad grows the green bits of it and the orange bits (which are carrots), and that's all I know.

There was going to be a 'wonderful' prize – a book (surprise!) – and Miss Felton called out two names at a time, because there are two in a team. She called out:

"Team One – Ron Tubman and John Tubman." (They're *always* put together.)

"Team Two – Lizzie Alexander and Tomas Flem.

"Team Three – Billy Williams and Roy Pawson.

"Team Four –

64

Jessica Jolly and Ann Fidgen."

It's not fair! Everyone on the list groaned. Open Day contests take *days* to get ready, and the people who have their names called out do all the work, the rest of the class can do what they like. It's not like five minutes spent covering a washing-up-liquid bottle with red tissue, sticking a feather on it and calling it a parrot! (That was the last thing Jessica Jolly and I did together. It was the stupidest-looking thing you've ever seen.) Now, we'd even have to work at the weekend. *Out of school.*

Still, at least I had Jessica Jolly as my partner. I knew we'd win. The other teams were rubbish. John and Ron have one brain between them. Billy Williams is the clumsiest person in the world – he can trip over a peanut. Roy Pawson is the school clown (except he doesn't make *me* laugh). Lizzie only thinks about exercising and sports, which is why her nose is on sideways because it was hit by a hockey stick. (It wasn't my fault she *moved*.) And Tomas looks like a squeeze of toothpaste, hardly able to stand up. What a bunch of losers.

"*Ea . . . sy . . . Ea . . . sy,*" I chanted. I didn't *want* to go in for the competition, but if I *had* to, I wanted to *win*!

We had a whole week to do something. The first thing we had to do was find out what the other teams were up to. After school, Jessica Jolly and I followed Team Two

to the Asian Shop in the main road, next to the launderette. But, actually, we couldn't go in without being seen, so we didn't find out what they were doing in there.

We spied on the others too.

Team One was collecting a pile of jam-jars. What were they going to do with jam-jars?

" ...or we could do something with Spanish food," we heard Ron say to John (from our snooping place in the book cupboard). "Like that stuff we had on holiday, *paella*."

"*Paella*? What's *paella*? I don't remember *paella*."

Ron said, "It's like rice pudding with shells in and octopuses' legs. And squids and stuff."

"That's dumb, Ron," said John. "Where're we going to get octopuses' legs and squids?"

They went out of the room then, still talking, and we crept out of our hiding place. Were the others going to cook real food? We'd

thought we'd get away with just some
photographs of food from different countries
and a display of old frying pans. We'd never
win against *real* food. We had to think again.

"What dishes from other countries do you
know?" I asked Jessica.

She had to think hard. "None," she said. "I
only know *British* food, like pizza and
hamburgers and alphabetti spaghetti ...
Kentucky Fried Chicken ... stuff like that."

"Well, we'll have to get help," I said.

"There's loads of kids in school whose mums and dads come from other countries. We could ask them what they eat."

"I've got a better idea," I said. "We could ask their mums if they'd *cook* something for us. And there's old Mr Kravitz next door to Gran. He's Polish. From Poland. I'll ask him as well."

It was easy, actually, because everyone we

asked was really pleased to help. Doctor
Kapoor, who is Tina's mum, Mr Pei, Mrs
Dhaliwal, Mrs Benevente and Mrs Tellapousis
all said they'd make something really cool
from the country their families came from
once. I also spoke to Mr Ravenelli, who's from
Scotland.

"Well now," Mr Ravenelli said to
me. "I shall make you my
masterpiece, the *haggis*! Do
you know what a haggis
is, lassie? It's a sheep's
stomach filled with ..."

And he told us what's
inside a haggis, which
is not actually very nice.
There are bits of fat and
guts and other stuff that
normal people put in the bin –
and porridge, and all the time
he was looking at us and
expecting us to go,
"Urgh! Gross!" but we
smiled sweetly and said,

"*Fab*, Mr Ravenelli. Sounds really lovely!"
Well . . . *we* didn't have to eat it, did we?

Then I went to Gran's. She was on her
hands and knees with her head in the
cupboard under the sink. There were bits of
pipes and tools all over the place. I asked her
bottom if she'd cook something for a school
project.

"Depends how long it takes – to put in
this – new boiler," she said. "And – change

the old radiators."

She sat back on her heels and her face was bright red due to bending over in a cupboard with a spanner.

"And put the pipes back and wire it all into the electric."

"You don't have to cook it *today*," I said.

"Oh well, then there's no problem," said Gran.

She promised to make us something really, really English – a 'Starry-Gazey Pie', whatever that is. "Hardly anyone eats it any more," she said. "But it's as English as the Queen."

Also, Mr Kravitz was making us 'Chlodnik' from sour cream and beetroot …

By then we knew the names of all the dishes we'd been promised. There was Chicken Tikka and Chow Mein, Couscous and Moussaka, Clam Chowder and Vichyssoise and lots of other stuff – every one from a different country. We asked a teacher to help us with the computer so we could make name-labels and proper menus and we printed them out. They looked brilliant. We put them

in a locker to keep what we were doing a
secret. And then we waited for Open Day.

★

Jessica Jolly and I were ready as soon as the
Egg-and-Spoon race finished and our
cooking people brought the food in. They'd
put everything in nice dishes. It was all going
really fantastically and the best part was that
all the hard work had been done by someone
else. We even had time to look around at
what the other teams were doing.

Team Three had a big poster in front of

their table announcing THE GREATEST
GRUB IN THE GALAXY.

Every bit of the Greatest Grub in the
Galaxy was on one plate: a sausage, a
hamburger, some baked beans and some
chips. *They* might have thought it was the
greatest grub in the galaxy, but it didn't seem
much on a big white plate on a big white
tablecloth, looking as if it had been cooked

last Thursday. Billy and Roy glared at us when they saw our huge table full of freshly cooked food and smelled the delicious smells.

Team Two, Lizzie and Tomas, had a better idea. THE WORLD'S WEIRDEST FOOD was written on their table poster. They had 'Ladies' Fingers', which were not ladies' fingers, but a vegetable. 'Toad in the Hole', which had no hole and no toad either, just

sausages. And 'Bombay Duck', which is a fish. It was *slightly* interesting, but we knew it was no match for our display, which we called: FREE FOOD HERE!

Then there was Team One, the Tubman twins, and their display of *jam labels*! It was the most pathetic thing we'd ever seen. So why were they so full of themselves, with evil smiles on their faces every time they looked over at us?

We soon found out.

When we got our printed food labels out of the locker ... *they'd all been changed*! Our printed stuff wasn't there any more. Instead, there were just bits of paper torn from an exercise book and written on with a felt-tipped pen to make new, badly-scrawled labels with names like *Bogeyburgers* and *Rat Crumble, Slug-Slime-Jelly and Custard* and *Pee Soup*!

That was when the parents chose to come in.

I could see my dad and Gran and Jessica Jolly's mum. They were still a long way from us, but Jessica Jolly was really freaked, staring

at the new labels with her mouth open. Honestly, she's so *wet*.

"Come on," I said. "Help me put these labels on. The people are coming in."

"But the names are awful!" she wailed. "We'll have to not label the food at all. And the printed labels looked so nice."

"We need *more* revolting names," I said. "There's not enough. We need more labels and we haven't got much time. Help me think some up. It'll be all right, you'll see."

While the parents were still smiling at the useless jam labels and ladies' fingers, we quickly wrote out some more disgusting labels and put them next to the plates of food. I made labels for *Sick on Toast* (that was for the pizza) and *Cowpats* (for the pancakes) and *Boiled Worms* (spaghetti). There was a bowl of something I didn't know. It was green and sort of gluey. I wrote 'Snot Soup'.

When I looked up, there was Miss Felton, looking ready to burst. "I'll speak to you later!" she snapped and stomped off.

Just then some of the parents came along, and one woman squealed, "Oh look, everyone, look at these fun dishes." And soon everyone was grabbing a plate and a fork or a spoon and stuffing their faces, saying things like, "Oh, you have *Hot Dog-Poo*. My favourite!" And, "I haven't had *Bogeyburgers* for years!" And, "Can I have some more of your delicious Snot Soup?"

The other teachers joined in then, tasting the Putrid Pudding, Stinky Stew, Smelly Jelly, Puffin Muffin and Whiffy Weasel Waffles. Miss

Felton was smiling about the 'brilliant idea' the parents were telling her it was, as if she'd thought it up herself. We told all the people who did the cooking what the Tubmans had done, so they wouldn't think we were making fun of the food, but they thought it was a laugh and enjoyed eating each other's cooking from other countries. Jessica Jolly's mum was allergic to foreign food and didn't eat *anything*. My dad was still eating ladies' fingers *from the enemy table*!

It was a mega success and we won the prize easily – a book about toadstools – and when everyone had finished eating every scrap, there was one dish that hadn't been touched –

Gran's Starry-Gazey Pie. And no wonder. It had three fishes' heads sticking up through the pastry, looking at us cross-eyed. It looked revolting.

Gran ate it all by herself.

And I went home and read about toadstools! (I didn't really.)